JUNIOR Dragster Science

My sincere thanks to the following people for their time, information, images and enthusiasm for this book:

Leanne Bernhard, Melbourne, Australia

Leanne Braggs, Melbourne, Australia

Ian Macarthur, Calder Park Raceway, Melbourne, Australia

Amy, Kelsey and their family, Auckland, New Zealand

Keiran and Malcolm Price, Hamilton, New Zealand

Arley, Emma, Mike and Jill Ballard, Illinois, the USA

Dear Reader

One day, I watched a TV report about people who drive dragcars. What really grabbed my interest in the story was the enthusiastic group of mothers and grandmothers who raced dragcars, and attended the Drag School at Calder Park Raceway in Melbourne, Australia. I also found out about children who race smaller versions of dragcars, called junior dragsters.

> 'OPERATION DRAG RIGHT' IS ONE WAY WE PROMOTE SAFETY AT DRAG-RACING TRACKS IN MELBOURNE.
>
> A VICTORIAN POLICE OFFICER

I started to research this fascinating sport, and I met three families who were passionate about supporting their kids' interest in racing junior dragsters. You will meet successful junior dragsters in New Zealand – Kieran Price, and sisters Amy Wilson and Kelsey Forbes. From Illinois, the USA, sisters Arley and Emma Ballard, known as Fast Chick Racing, will share their racing secrets.

The final chapter returns to Melbourne, where you'll find out why two friends Leanne Bernhard (a mum) and Leanne Braggs (a grandmother) enjoy competing against each other on the racetrack.

I hope you enjoy the inspiring stories behind the scenes of drag racing and junior dragsters.

Sharon Parsons

Contents

JUNIOR Dragster Science

1 What Is Dragcar Racing?

Dragcar racing is the world's fastest acceleration motorsport on the shortest racetrack. Dragcar racing has many different race classes, based on types of vehicles, and junior dragster racing has just two age-based divisions.

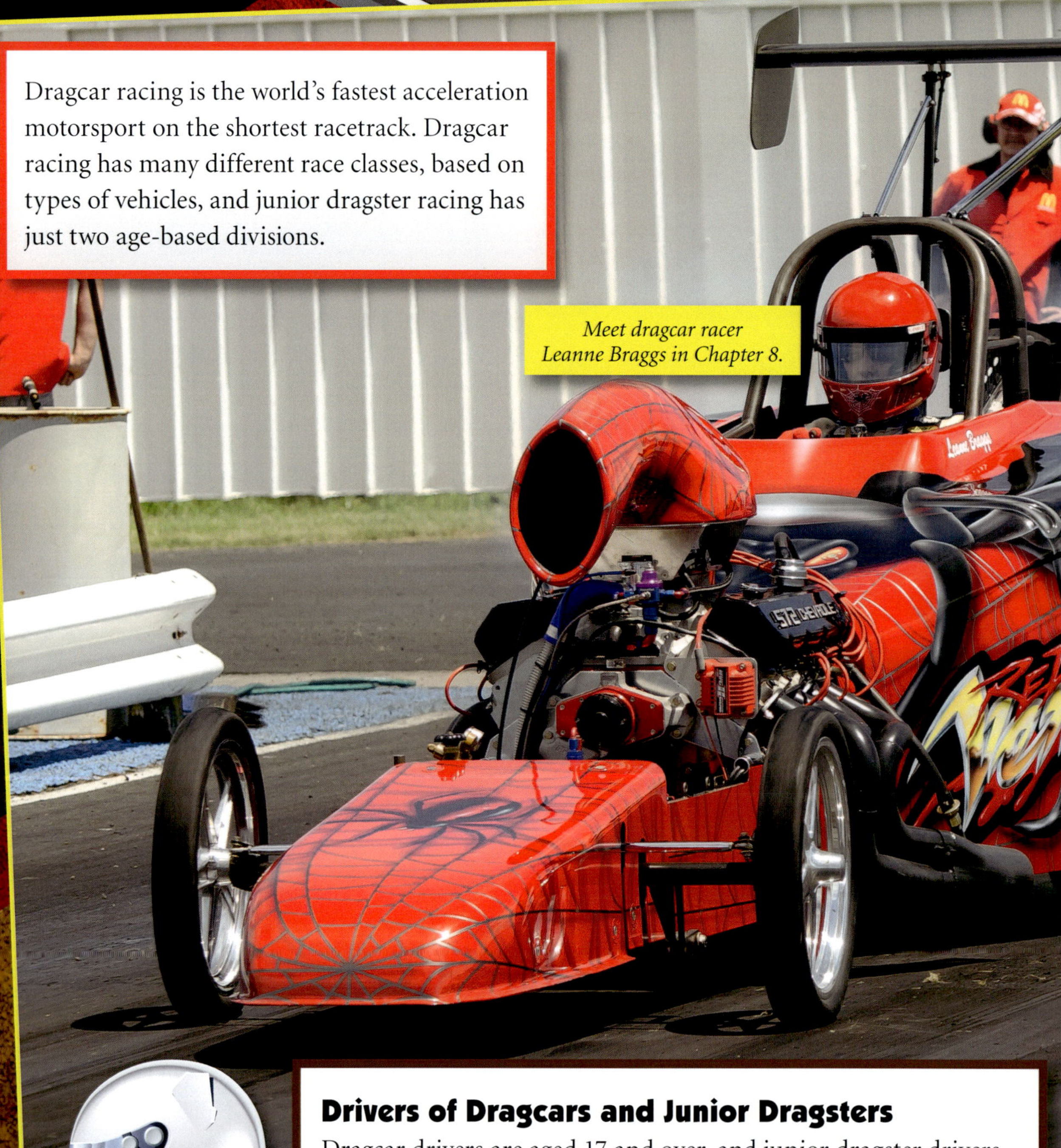

Meet dragcar racer Leanne Braggs in Chapter 8.

Drivers of Dragcars and Junior Dragsters

Dragcar drivers are aged 17 and over, and junior dragster drivers can be from eight to 16 years of age. They are all highly trained competitors who race high-performance, modified vehicles at extreme velocity in races that usually last for less than ten seconds!

A Junior Dragster

A junior dragster is a less powerful replica of a dragcar, designed for use by younger drivers. But these modified vehicles are still very fast!

Meet junior dragster Kelsey Forbes in Chapter 5.

History

Junior Dragsters Start in New Zealand

In 1988, a new kind of drag racing for kids was introduced, first known as midget dragster racing. Soon after, the sport became popular in countries such as Australia and the USA, and then Junior Dragster became an international class of competition.

Racetrack **Safety**

Safety is paramount at every dragcar racetrack. Prior to every race day, track and race officials check the quality and safety of the track.

The Calder Park Raceway stand has clear signage for first aid assistance.

Race officials check the dragcar racetrack.

A tractor smooths out any uneven areas of the track's surface.

The Police in "Operation Drag Right"

A team of police officers race dragcars as part of a drag-racing safety program called "Operation Drag Right". Their presence at the dragcar racing tracks helps to promote the message of safety.

police dragcars

ready to drive to the racetrack

last safety check inside the dragcar

Driver Safety

Meet Arley Ballard (left) and Emma Ballard (right) in Chapter 7 – they are junior dragster competitors in the USA.

Dragcars Scrutineered

Drivers must complete training courses, and their cars are carefully checked, or scrutineered, by race officials before and after each race. The rules for all competitors and their dragcars are very strict.

The scrutineer carefully checks the dragcar so that it is safe to race.

Before the race, Datto, the driver, waits with her friends while her dragcar is scrutineered.

2 The Dragcar Racetrack

1/8 mile: 0.25 miles x 1.61 = 0.4025 km

1/4 mile: 0.125 miles x 1.61 = 0.2013 km

Christmas Tree Lights

Left Lane Burnout Area

Right Lane Burnout Area

Race Track (Distance is either 1/8 mile or 1/4 mile)

Pre-Stage Beam

Stage Beam

Guard Beam

The "Christmas Tree" Lights

A set of lights, known as "Christmas tree" lights, control each dragcar race, and signal when each of the two competitors can start. The two adjacent columns of lights are linked to a computer system, and they tell each driver what to do in the pre-race stages. Drag-racing drivers concentrate hard on their lights – if they make a mistake, they're disqualified.

Pre-Stage Lights

The first light flashes on to alert each driver that they are getting close to the staging beam (an infrared beam).

Staging lights

The next light flashes on to inform the driver to slowly move the front wheels across the staging beam, but they must stop at the guard beam.

Guard Beam

Once the car crosses over this final infrared beam, the race timer starts for each car.

Amber Lights

Three amber lights flash in succession to alert the driver that the green light will flash on in less than a second.

Green Light

The driver can start the race when they see the green light flash on.

The "Cherry" Light

When drivers cross the guard beam while the orange lights are still flashing, a red light, or "cherry" light, flashes and they are disqualified from racing for the day.

pre-stage beam (left), staging beam (middle), guard beam (right)

a 1950s modified Chevrolet capable of speeds of up to 289 kilometres an hour

Measurements in Drag Racing

The sport of drag racing began in the USA in the 1950s. The USA uses imperial measurements, and this is a tradition that has remained in drag racing. A drag-racing track is either an eighth of a mile (about 0.201 kilometres) or a quarter of a mile (about 0.402 kilometres) in length. Even outside the USA, dragcar competitors use imperial measurements. Many racers who live in other parts of the world import vehicles or engines from the USA, so they need to think in imperial, rather than metric, terms.

Distance Measurements – Imperial and Metric

SHORT DISTANCE UNITS OF MEASUREMENTS		LONG DISTANCE UNITS OF MEASUREMENTS	
IMPERIAL	METRIC	IMPERIAL	METRIC
FEET	METRES	MILES	KILOMETRES

CONVERT FEET TO METRES

To convert feet to metres, multiply the number of feet by 0.3048 to get the equivalent in metres.

1 foot x 0.3048
= 0.3048 metres

CONVERT MILES TO KILOMETRES

To convert miles to kilometres, multiply the number of miles by 1.61 to get the equivalent in kilometres.

1 mile x 1.61
= 1.61 kilometres

3 Maths Is Important

All dragcar and junior dragster drivers recognise the importance of maths in the sport. There are many instances where they must make calculations.

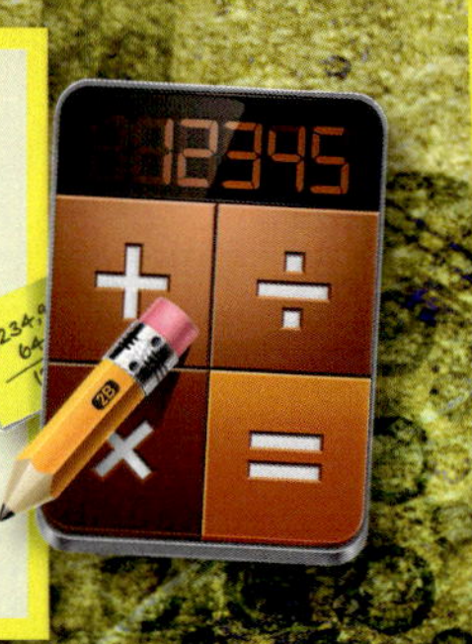

calculating a dial-in time to be put on the car's plate

1. Calculate

Dial-In Racing Times

Before each race, drivers submit their dial-in time to the race organisers. Junior dragsters only race over an eighth of a mile track. Each driver needs to ensure that they provide race officials with a dial-in time that is close to the car's proven performance times in the past. One method of working out dial-in times is to calculate the average of the driver's last three race times.

	Previous Race Times (seconds)
Dragcar Driver 1	1st time: 7.39
	2nd time: 7.37
	3rd time: 7.35
	Total = 22.11
Dragcar Driver 2	1st time: 9.47
	2nd time: 9.42
	3rd time: 9.66
	Total = 28.55

Calculate the average for Dragcar Driver 1 to work out the new dial-in time:

Total divided by 3 = 7.37 seconds

Calculate the average for Dragcar Driver 2 to work out the new dial-in time:

Total divided by 3 = 9.52 seconds

Based on the calculation below, the Christmas tree lights for Junior Dragster Driver 1 will count down to the green light 2.14 seconds ahead of the green light for Junior Dragster Driver 2.

2. Calculate

Handicap Equations

Drivers try to calculate the right dial-in time because they don't want to give their opponent an advantage when racing in the handicap race system. A simplified example of how the handicap race system works for two competing drivers is given below.

Junior Dragster Driver 2's New Dial-in Time of 9.51 seconds

Minus

Junior Dragster Driver 1's New Dial-in Time of 7.37 seconds

Equals

2.14 seconds

Therefore ... at the start of the next race, Junior Dragster Driver 1 gets a 2.14-second head start over Junior Dragster Driver 2.

So ... both competitors should reach the finish line around the same time!

And ... if both drivers cross the finish line at their exact dial-in times, the winner is the driver who posted the best reaction time when their green light flashed at the start.

Reaction Times

In dragcar racing, the reaction time is the time it takes for a driver to react to the green light and start racing hard. A perfect reaction time is 0.000, which means that there was no time between the green light flashing on and the junior dragster starting the race.

Arley Ballard (11 years old) posted her first perfect reaction time of 0.000 in 2011. It helped her to achieve her first win ever with her lowest (or quickest) race time of 8.900 seconds over a distance of an eighth of a mile! Read more about Arley in Chapter 7.

Technology

Elapsed Time (ET) and Speed

At the end of each race, two separate measurements of racing performance are recorded for each driver: elapsed time and speed. The elapsed time is the time it takes for the dragcar to complete the race distance. When a dragster leaves the starting line, the guard beam activates an elapsed-time clock, which stops when the car crosses the finish line. The speed is recorded at two different points along the track.

A Fair Sport for All

The most powerful cars driven by the most experienced drivers don't always win dragcar races. This is because each competitor must finish their race as close to their own dial-in time as possible. The dial-in time is the amount of time the driver estimates they will take to complete the race. Minutes before every race, dragcar drivers calculate their dial-in time and give it to race officials. For example, a driver who estimates a dial-in time of nine seconds, and then completes the race in nine seconds, can still beat a competing driver with a faster dial-in time of seven seconds, but who completes the race in eight seconds.

4 Science in Dragcar Racing

Side by side, two dragcars roll up slowly into the burnout area. Without warning, their engines roar with ear-piercing sounds and their wheels spin but the dragcars do not leave the short section of track. These are called "burnouts".

The Science of Burnouts

As the wheels spin faster, the rubber on the tyres gets extremely hot and sticky. The stickier tyres enable the dragcar to gain traction, which prevents the car from spinning out of control as it accelerates along the track.

Leanne Braggs does a burnout at the start of the track.

Weather Affects a Dial-In Time

Many weather and track factors influence the dial-in calculation. For example, a combination of two helpful conditions, a tailwind and a hot track, and one not-so-helpful condition, high humidity in the air, can affect the driver's dial-in time. So the driver must think about:

- the tailwind that will help to "push" the car
- the hot, sticky, rubbery track that will help to provide the tyres with greater traction for faster acceleration and speed
- high humidity that can "slow" an engine – an engine is more powerful in cooler temperatures.

Handheld Weather Stations

Many drivers use a handheld device called a "weather station" to input data, such as track- and wind-speed conditions, plus their previous race times. The device will calculate a dial-in speed based on the data keyed in. The driver must still make the final judgement because the barometer may show that conditions will soon change. A weather-station device can also alert drivers about weather warnings, such as:

falling barometric pressure – a falling pressure may indicate that rain is imminent. If the racetrack is wet, dragcar racing events are cancelled.

changing air temperature – in cold conditions, drivers need to do a longer burnout to warm up the tyres, but on a hotter day they will do a shorter burnout because the track is already hot and sticky.

unsafe levels of dew – this is a measure of the amount of moisture in the air and the temperature at which dew will form. Too much dew on the track can make the track unsafe.

Leanne Bernhard uses her weather station – meet Leanne in Chapter 8.

DEW

Dew is made up of tiny droplets of water and forms when the air cools and the water vapour in the air condenses.

Extreme Forces of Acceleration

Experienced dragcar drivers understand how the right design of the car and its engine can assist quicker acceleration. After each race they analyse how their car performed in all kinds of weather and track conditions. This knowledge helps them to feel more confident to race competitively, yet safely, on race day.

ACCELERATION AND VELOCITY

"Acceleration" is the term used to describe an increase of speed, or velocity. "Velocity" refers to the rate of motion.

Forces on the Body

When racing extremely fast, dragcar drivers feel the forces of high velocity on their bodies, as well as on their dragcars.

When a dragcar driver plants their foot down hard on their car's accelerator pedal, the car's speed increases quickly; the **g-force** is so great that their body is pushed back against their seat.

extreme acceleration on the dragcar racetrack

G-Force

The "g" in g-force stands for "gravitational". "G-force" refers to the force exerted on a body by gravity or when the body is accelerated. The g-force acting on a stationary object on Earth at sea level is 1 g, and is equal and opposite to gravity. The g-force exerted on an accelerating object, such as a dragster, is much greater.

What Is Gravity?

All objects exert a force that attracts other objects. Unless the object is the size of a planet, this attractive force, which we call gravity, is usually too tiny to be noticed. The gravity of Earth can be measured by how fast an object moves towards it. If we take away air resistance, anything that is dropped on Earth accelerates towards Earth's surface at 9.8 metres per second squared (or 9.8 m/s2). This means that the dropped object increases its velocity by 9.8 metres per second for each second of its descent. In a famous experiment conducted on the Moon, where there is no air resistance, a feather and a hammer dropped by the crew of Apollo 15 both landed on the Moon's surface at exactly the same rate and time.

Drivers feel powerful g-forces at extreme acceleration.

Racing Force

A driver inside an accelerating dragcar will feel the effect, or weight, of a powerful g-force. To remain safe, a driver must be firmly restrained in their seat because any movement at this extreme acceleration could cause harm to their body.

Stopping Force

The same principle applies when the dragcar driver must quickly stop the car at the end of the racetrack by using the brakes or releasing a parachute from the rear of the car. The decelerating force is so great that a driver can be dangerously thrust forwards if they are not tightly secured in their seat.

An astronaut in space feels zero g-force.

Earth Science

An Astronaut Feels Zero G-Force

An astronaut inside an orbiting spacecraft feels zero g-force because in space there is no gravity and, as such, people experience a feeling of weightlessness.

Examples of G-Force

Standing on Earth at sea level	1 g
Space shuttle during launch and re-entry	3 g
Formula One car, under maximum braking	5+ g

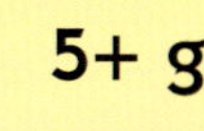

Physical Science

A Parachutist Feels Minimal G-Force

When a parachutist freefalls against gravity, they feel minimal g-forces because of other forces, called "drag forces". Therefore, a parachutist experiences a feeling of being "supported" by the air.

A parachutist feels minimal g-forces.

5 Sisters Race Junior Dragsters in New Zealand

Kelsey Forbes

Kelsey Forbes was only six years old when she began junior dragster racing at the Meremere track in New Zealand. At that time, she raced in the junior class for six-to-eight-year-olds, but in 2011, the New Zealand Drag Racing Association abolished her class. She was only seven, and Kelsey had to be eight years old to qualify for the newly formed junior class. However, because she was such an experienced driver, the New Zealand Drag Racing Association allowed her to race in the eight-to-12-year-old class. Kelsey's eighth birthday was in February 2012.

Amy Wilson

Amy Wilson is Kelsey's older sister, and she began racing at the age of eleven, in 2005. She is one of New Zealand's top female junior dragster racers, and her many trophies are symbols of her success. Like most junior dragster racers, Amy loves the excitement she feels when she races extremely fast.

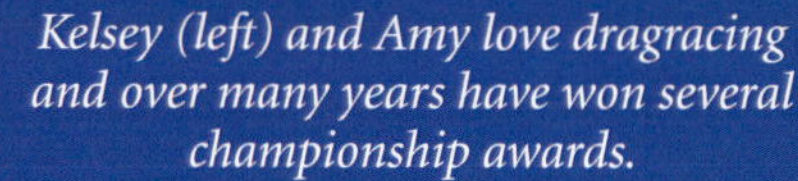

Kelsey (left) and Amy love dragracing and over many years have won several championship awards.

Sisters Race against Each Other

Amy and Kelsey have raced each other several times – even though Kelsey's dial-in time is around 14.1 seconds and Amy's time is faster at 8.9 seconds. Amy explains, "With the handicap system, Kelsey was given a 5.2-second head start and it was psychologically hard to wait and watch my little sister's car a long way ahead of me.

"All I could do was rev up my car until my green light flashed and then I planted my foot down hard on the accelerator. After that race, I felt bad because Kelsey had tears in her eyes when I beat her by a thousandth of a second."

But the sisters know that one day it could all change!

An Interview With Amy Wilson

Q: How did you get started in junior dragster racing?

A: At the drag-racing track, my dad asked me to sit in my brother's dragcar to see if I liked it. As I sat there, I began imagining what it would feel like to race, and thought it could be fun!

Q: What happened next?

A: A couple of weeks later, my dad really surprised me when a truck pulled up outside our house with a dragcar on it.

Q: Why do you love junior dragster racing?

A: I love the adrenaline rush and the speed! I always want to get down that track as fast as possible.

Q: What is your best ET (elapsed time)?

A: It's 8.9 seconds.

Q: How has dragster racing changed you?

A: It has definitely made me feel more confident because this sport is about personal effort. It's about how well *you* perform, not the car.

Amy's **Race Strategy**

Amy before the Race

1. Burnout Area

WARM-UP ENGINE: Amy slowly rolls her car through the wet area at the start of the burnout area and focuses on the lights and the track ahead. Occasionally she does a burnout to warm up her tyres.

2. Pre-Staged Area

FOCUS: Amy focuses to clear her head of any distractions while she waits for the amber lights to begin flashing.

3. Pre-Staged Area

REV ENGINE: Amy likes to rev up the engine to a very loud 16 000 revs to warm it up and psychologically challenge her opponent in the next lane.

Mathematics

What Are "Revs"?

"Revs" stands for "revolutions", which is short for revolutions per minute (RPM). This measurement term tells how many times per minute an engine rotates, and is used to indicate engine speed. In a car engine, 6 000 revs is a low engine speed; 16 000 revs is very fast and usually very loud.

4. Pre-Staged Area

FOCUS ON AMBER LIGHTS: Amy focuses on the Christmas tree lights facing her lane. When all three amber lights have flashed in sequence, Amy knows that her green light will flash four-tenths of a second later so her right foot rests gently on the accelerator.

5. Staged Beam at the Start Line

FOCUS ON GREEN LIGHT: As soon as the green light comes on, Amy reacts quickly, planting the accelerator to the floor and racing towards the finish line.

Amy during the Race

Timer Starts

Amy's race timer starts when the green light comes on.

Speed Trap Timer Records

The speed trap covers the last 66 feet (20.12 metres) of the race before the finish line and it computes the top speed for Amy's car.

Elapsed Time (ET) Beam at the Finish Line

Amy's elapsed time (race time) is recorded when her car crosses the last infrared beam at the finish line.

Amy after the Race

Shutdown Area

After Amy crosses the finish line, she takes her foot off the accelerator and brakes hard to slow down to a safe speed for driving back to the pits.

Time Sheet

On her way to the pits, Amy collects her time sheet from the race officials.
It lists her elapsed time, reaction time and terminal speed (top speed).

Evaluate the Race

After every race Amy discusses her time sheet and any car problems with her parents.

A Top Junior Dragster in New Zealand

In 2011, Kieran Price became New Zealand's top junior dragster when he finished the six-month competition. He was only 14 years old.

Since he started racing at the age of six, Kieran has developed a passion for the sport and won many junior dragster competitions.

Kieran says, "Dragster racing is a part of my life, I've been brought up around dragsters. I used to get nervous when I first started racing but my confidence is much better now. I love driving dragsters because it's a fast, competitive sport and the experience sets me up for when I get my road licence in a couple of years."

Kieran's new junior dragster was imported from the USA.

Kieran's new car has an engine that's double the size of his previous junior dragster.

A Dragracing Family

Many junior dragster racers have grown up with dragcar racing as a family sport. In Kieran's case, his father and uncle built and raced dragcars, so it seemed inevitable that he would follow in their footsteps.

Kieran and his father Malcolm attend every race together.

Kieran's Best Results

By the end of the 2011 race season, Kieran's best racing results were:

Elapsed Time		7.900 seconds
Reaction Time		0.002 seconds

WHEN I SAY THAT MY 'ET' WAS '790', MY MATES KNOW THAT IT MEANS 7.900 SECONDS

KIERAN PRICE

Kieran also enjoys "driving" the ride-on mower!

7 Sisters Race Junior Dragsters in the USA

Fast Chick Racing

Emma Ballard is 16 years old and her sister Arley is 11 years old. They are junior dragster racers in Illinois, the USA. In Illinois, the winter weather brings snow and the occasional blizzard, so the racing season is between spring and autumn (April to October).

Emma (left) and Arley Ballard work hard to keep their junior dragster in peak condition.

Emma Ballard's helmet

Sisters Share a Car

The sisters share one car, so they each race for one half of the race season. They can't race the same car on the same day because many adjustments need to be made to suit their different heights, such as altering the steering wheel and the pedals.

Arley helps her father Mike to get Emma ready for her race.

Sponsorship

Junior Dragster racing is an expensive sport, so Emma and Arley's father suggested that they write letters to companies to ask for sponsorship. A company that makes air filters for dragcar engines now covers some of their racing costs.

Arley and Emma take a break from racing.

Arley's Thank-You Letter

Dear Mr. Harris,
I just wanted to write you a thank you letter. My sister and I are really excited having K&N Filters sponsor us. We hope we will do a good job for you and make you proud of our team. My dad said he bought his first K&N filter back in 1986. I can't wait to start racing. We have decals everywhere. Hope you like the newspaper article. Thank you again
love Arley!
Arley Ballard

a copy of the letter written to the air filter company that helps to sponsor Arley and Emma's car

the Fast Chick junior dragster engine

Arley Answers

HER FIRST RACE: "I felt nervous, a little scared and had butterflies, and my knees were shaking against the controls, but after the race I felt happy and very excited!"

PERFECT REACTION TIME 0.000: "I didn't realise it was that good, I didn't even mean to do it!"

ABOUT WINNING: "I haven't won yet, but it's not about winning, it's about having fun as I love going really fast!"

Arley Speeds Up in Two Years

NINE YEARS OLD: Arley's fastest speed was 55 miles/hour (88.55 km/h) and her quickest ET was 10.3 seconds.

ELEVEN YEARS OLD: Arley's fastest speed was 71 miles/hour (114.31 km/h) and her quickest ET was 8.9 seconds.

Emma Answers

PRE-RACE BREAKFAST: "I love waffles with peanut butter!"

LEARN FROM THE PROFESSIONALS: "I love to watch how the professional racers get ready for a good start at the Christmas tree."

LEARN MECHANICS OF THE CAR: "I started an automechanics course at school because my teacher said I should know how to fix my car. I wasn't excited at first, but now I can see how it can help me work better with Dad when we fix the car."

RACE FEELING: "I feel butterflies before the race but once I'm racing (with all the windows up) it feels awesome! After the race, I put on the air conditioning, quick!"

> "I HAVEN'T WON A RACE YET BUT I STILL LOVE COMPETING."
>
> EMMA

Emma waits to race while Arley helps Mike make some final adjustments to the junior dragster.

Emma prepares for the race ahead.

Emma's Best Results (1/8–mile track)

Fastest ET	82.11 miles/hour
Best Reaction Time	0.111 seconds

Dad Always Helps

Emma and Arley appreciate the long hours that their father Mike puts in to maintain and fix their junior dragster at home and at the track. One way that the girls help their father is to hand him the numbered pieces when he is assembling parts of the car at the racetrack. And if they need extra help or a new part at the track, there is always someone ready to help out. The Ballard family enjoy the sense of fair play and camaraderie at the track.

Emma observes how her father works on an engine part.

THE GIRLS DON'T GET A FREE RIDE, THEY HELP OUT.

MIKE BALLARD

Emma puts her hands over her ears when her father tests the engine.

What Does Mum Think?

Jill is the mother of Emma and Arley. When asked what she thinks about her daughters racing junior dragsters, she replies, "It has taught the girls to be humble in defeat and I enjoy seeing them have fun because they LOVE it! If they had an accident, I know that they would be safer in their junior dragster than in the school bus. The dragster safety rules are very strict."

THE STARTING LINE BRINGS OUT THE BUTTERFLIES, THE ADRENALINE RUSH AND THE TEARY EYES.

JILL BALLARD

Jill Ballard wishes Arley well for her race.

8 Mums and Grandmothers Race, Too!

Two Leannes Love Dragcar Racing

Leanne Bernhard and Leanne Braggs are friends, but on the racetrack, they are competitors!

Leanne Bernhard has learnt how her engine works and how to maintain its high-performance condition.

Leanne Bernhard

Leanne Bernhard is a successful drag-racing driver who lives in Melbourne, Australia. She is the mother of three children and her husband is a drag-racing driver, too. Leanne volunteers her time to teach at the Drag School, Calder Park Raceway in Melbourne. She is one of three directors at the Australian Women's Motor Sport Network (AWMN).

Leanne Bernhard's dragcar

"WE CALL OURSELVES 'QUEENS OF SPEED'"

LEANNE BERNHARD

Drag Racing Is a Sport

Leanne Bernhard is passionate about drag racing. She says that people often confuse the sport of drag racing with street racing. Street racing is illegal and dangerous because people race on public roads.

Leanne Braggs

Leanne Braggs is a wife, mother and grandmother who also happens to be a champion drag-racing driver at the top level of this high-acceleration sport.

> "I FIRST THOUGHT DRAGCAR RACING WAS A RIDICULOUS SPORT! WHO WOULD WANT TO WATCH TWO CARS RACE IN A STRAIGHT LINE? BUT AFTER FIVE YEARS OF RACING, I LOVE IT!"
>
> LEANNE BRAGGS

Leanne with her first dragcar which she raced in the Top Eliminator Class

Leanne in her new dragcar, which she races in the Modified Class

Leanne Catches the Drag-Racing Bug

For many years Leanne Braggs enjoyed playing in golf competitions, but in 2006 that all changed when she sat in her son's dragcar. Leanne began to imagine what it would be like to compete in drag racing and win. The following week, Leanne attended the Drag School at Calder Park Raceway, and met Leanne Bernhard. Soon after, she bought her first dragcar and today, Leanne is one of the sport's most formidable competitors and often wins!

Leanne's Maths Mind

Leanne says that she is continually working out equations in her head when she is at the dragcar racetrack. She is able to instantly recall her best race results, such as the ones below when she won a significant dragcar race in 2011.

Leanne drives from the parking area to the dragcar racetrack.

Leanne's Best Results, 1/8-Mile Track

	DIAL-IN (SECONDS)	ACTUAL RACE TIME (SECONDS)	REACTION TIME (SECONDS)
1ST ELIMINATION RACE	5.200	5.210	0.005
2ND ELIMINATION RACE	5.150	5.180	0.000
3RD ELIMINATION RACE	5.150	5.152	0.020
FINAL RACE	5.150	5.180	0.009

Leanne's Best Results, 1/4-Mile Track

- Best Reaction Time → 0.000 seconds
- Fastest Time → 7.940 seconds
- Fastest Speed → 169 miles/hour (272 km/hour)

Leanne waits while her husband Steve finishes work on the back wheel.

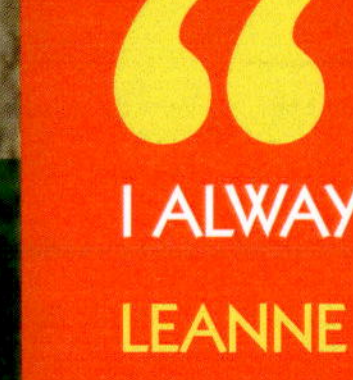

> "I ALWAYS LOVED MATHS AT SCHOOL."
>
> LEANNE BRAGGS

EXPOSITION FEATURE

Women in Drag Racing

DRAGCAR INSIGHT NEWS

TEXT TYPE
Exposition

By
Sue Gray

Over the years I have met some people who think that females should not, or cannot, compete against men on the drag-racing track. However, in my experience, women are suited to the physical and mental challenges of the sport. They are equally as capable as men to compete – and win – in the sport of drag racing.

First, recent scientific studies have shown that women have very fast reaction times. It is important for every drag-racing driver to have a fast reaction time. This ability helps them to accelerate quickly from the starting line – a drag race is won or lost by reacting quickly at the start of a race. I believe that because women have reaction times that are at least as fast as men's reaction times, they can challenge and beat male drivers in the sport of drag racing. Knowing they have this advantage gives female racers the confidence to be successful in this sport.

Second, drag-racing cars and gear are individually designed to suit drivers. This gives each driver the optimal fit-out, regardless of his or her strength, body type and ability. With the right car and gear designed to match her body size and racing ability, a female driver can compete successfully against all drivers – men and other women alike.

Third, women make good dragracers because the sport does not require superior physical endurance – drag-racing drivers compete over a track that is about 403 metres long. With such a short track, a drag race does not require the endurance of other car-racing sports, like V8 supercars, for example; rather, a drag race is over in a few seconds. Women and men are equally equipped to handle these conditions.

Last, women and men are equally capable of learning all of the safety aspects of drag racing. Once a female racer completes an appropriate safety course, she has the knowledge necessary to drive in accordance with the race rules, as fast as possible, and safely, against other competitors, regardless of whether they are men or women.

In conclusion, I believe that women can compete against men in drag racing. Women's fast reaction times, the modifications that can be made to the drag-racing cars, and the fact that a drag race is a short race, all mean that women have the same, if not better, ability as men to perform in this exciting sport.

Index

Glossary

acceleration The rate at which the speed of something is increasing

adrenaline A substance produced by the body in a response to stress or excitement which results in increased heartbeat

camaraderie The feeling of trust and close friendship between a group of people

g-force The force exerted on the body when it is accelerated

handicap A disadvantage or advantage given to competitors according to their skill

infrared Electromagnetic radiation with wavelengths longer than visible light but shorter than radio waves

modified Changed slightly in order to improve it

pits Areas at the side of a track where cars can be serviced and refuelled during a race

revs Shortened form of "revolutions"; to speed up an engine by pressing the accelerator but without engaging the gears so that the engine remains stationary

velocity The speed at which something is moving in a particular direction